T0271547

Praise for *Zenith Hotel*, winner of the Prix de Flore, 2012

'Oscar Coop-Phane oozes affection for his characters, from their beautiful humanity to the depths of their weaknesses' *Huffington Post*

'One of the most intriguing and exciting new voices on the French literary scene' *Seymour* magazine

'The best first novel of the year' *Le Parisien*

'He's only 23, but Coop-Phane's sparse style cuts to the bone and reveals a sensibility far beyond his years' *Le Point*

'A melancholic and earthy novel that marks a rigorous, vigorous entrance into contemporary French literature' *Le Figaro*

'Coop-Phane has achieved the modest and moving prose of Calet and Bove – not a copier, but an extraordinary amateur paying tribute to his readings. His poetic text is as sad as a lonely Sunday' *Télérama*

'*Zenith Hotel* is a melancholy portrait of desire and radiant grace' Olivier Mony, *Sud Ouest*

'In this astonishing first novel, Coop-Phane has brought alive the inhabitants of the dirty, poor streets of Paris, compiling a spare yet tender portrait that is never sentimental. An unbelievable discovery' Coline Hugel, *Page des libraires*

'It's beautiful. It's sad. It's pure poetry' Eva Bester, *28 minutes*

'A short and thought-provoking book that lays bare the unvarnished heart of city dwelling. It's populated by people trying to manage their lives, and their footsteps reverberate across the hard tarmac of the arrondissements – the unforgiving structure that underpins each vignette. Astutely observed and told with care' @tripfiction

'*Zenith Hotel* is pure poetry. It's a one-sitting read that manages to fit more emotion into 105 pages than most novels do in 500' Amanda Horan @gobookyourselfx

Zenith Hotel

ABOUT THE AUTHOR

Oscar Coop-Phane was born in 1988. He left home at 16 with dreams of becoming a painter and at 20 moved to Berlin where he spent a year writing and reading classics. There he wrote *Zenith Hotel*, which won the Prix de Flore in France, and then *Tomorrow, Berlin* (Arcadia, 2015). Today he lives in Brussels and is working on his third novel, *October*.

ABOUT THE TRANSLATOR

Over the last three decades Ros Schwartz has translated a wide range of Francophone authors including Arcadia's Dominique Manotti (whose *Lorraine Connection* won the 2008 International Dagger Award). In 2009 the French government made her *Chevalier de l'Ordre des Arts et des Lettres* for her services to literature.

Zenith Hotel

Oscar Coop-Phane

Translated from the French by Ros Schwartz

ARCADIA BOOKS

Arcadia Books Ltd
139 Highlever Road
London W10 6PH

www.arcadiabooks.co.uk

First published in France by Éditions Finitude 2012
First published in the United Kingdom by Arcadia Books 2014

A catalogue record for this book is available from the British Library.

ISBN 978-1-909807-50-1

Typeset by MacGuru Ltd
Printed and bound by CPI Group (UK) Ltd., Croydon CR0 4YY

This book is supported by the Institut Français (Royaume-
Uni) as part of the Burgess programme. Arcadia Books
would like to thank them for their generous support.

Arcadia Books supports English PEN *www.englishpen.org* and
The Book Trade Charity *http://booktradecharity.wordpress.com*

Arcadia Books distributors are as follows:

in the UK and elsewhere in Europe:
Macmillan Distribution Ltd
Brunel Road
Houndmills
Basingstoke
Hants RG21 6XS

in the USA and Canada:
Dufour Editions
PO Box 7
Chester Springs
PA 19425

in Australia/New Zealand:
NewSouth Books
University of New South Wales
Sydney NSW 2052

When I wake up, my teeth feel furry. There's a foul taste in my mouth – a nasty sort of animal taste. Still, it's better than at night, when I have the aftertaste of other people and their filth. My body is a hindrance. It spreads out on my sheets like a poorly inflated old sack. I try not to touch this sick body too much, too many hands have pawed it. It needs to rest a little longer in my grubby sheets.

I smoke in bed. Sometimes the ash drops on to the sheets making little grey smudges which I don't bother to rub away. I sleep with my ashes, like in a casket.

In the mornings, my nails ache. The tips of my fingers are cold, slightly numb. Apparently it's the alcohol. Whatever.

My hair's greasy and it sticks to the back of my neck.

I sit up a little. Feathers escape from my pillow when I move it, fluttering gently down on to the white-tiled floor. I lean back against the wall, scratch my head then light a cigarette. To wash it down, I drink a little water from the old plastic bottle lying at the foot of my bed, which I fill every night from the little sink on the landing.

I don't have a proper bed. I sleep on a sofa bed. I don't bother to fold it away any more.

～

Then, I have to go and pee. The toilet's on the landing, and I have to put on my shoes because the floor's wet. It's not a proper toilet, just a hole in the ground with two little white ceramic footrests. People say that in Turkey, you always have to shit crouching down. You have to squat in a ridiculous position over these toilets, too. My pee makes a loud tinkling sound as it hits the water, and that makes me laugh. I pull the little chain hanging from the huge cistern. You have to watch out – sometimes the water splashes your ankles.

I go back to my room, dragging my feet on the hexagonal red tiles. The door's open – I never close it when I go to the toilet. If someone came in, I'd hear them.

I splash my face at the sink on the landing and then wipe it with the hem of my nightie. It's a bit torn, but I like to feel its roughness against my skin. There's something sort of pure about it. The men don't see it.

～

I never start the day without a coffee. At night, when I run out, I walk to the store on Place Clichy to buy some more. Coffee's expensive there and I have to go up Rue d'Amsterdam. That's how badly I need caffeine in the morning.

～ 2 ～

Before, I used to have it sitting at the bar at Jeannot's. Always cheerful is Jeannot – always cracking jokes. He lost his wife in an accident. He smiles when he talks about her, remembering the good times, her little feminine ways. And there are the guys – small-time delinquents, lost souls, the old men from the neighbourhood. All on Pernod or white wine. But you can't smoke at Jeannot's any more, and I need a fag with my coffee, so I've stopped going there. I did tell Jeannot why, but he doesn't believe me. He thinks I'm going to another joint, the competition he calls it. He says I'm too stuck-up for his place, that I'm being a princess. When I walk past, he acts like he doesn't see me. It's really sad, this business, these anti-smoking laws. Lulu, my neighbour, she still goes there. She's the one who told me Jeannot thinks I'm being a princess.

⁓

I drink my coffee all alone in my room, smoking my fags. To cheer myself up, I tell myself I'm saving money.

I've got an Italian coffee pot, a metal cafetière. You put in the water, the coffee, and then you screw on the top part. When it boils, you have to take the cafetière off the cooker. I've got an electric hotplate. It's covered in grease and stinks a bit when you turn it on, but it still works. Maybe one day I'll buy a new one.

I drink my coffee and smoke a cigarette. No TV, no radio. I listen to the sound of the tobacco sizzling when I take a drag. It's relaxing. I try not to think. I've moved the table next to my bed. I sit there, puffing away and drinking coffee.

～

I get up, take a towel from the chest of drawers and go to my neighbour Lulu's. I haven't got a shower. She lets me use hers, and it's nicer. Before, I had to use the shared bathroom. No lock on the door, just a dribble of water and filthy floor tiles. We've asked the landlord to replace them hundreds of times, but he doesn't want to know. He says, *Isn't it enough that I rent out rooms to people like you? So get off my case.* He never wants us on his case, except when it's to pay the rent. He wants to know about that all right, the bastard. I know, everyone has to make a living … but that's still no reason to be such a shit.

His eyes are wide-set, like a fish, and he's bald. He taps his pudgy fingers on his counter and says he's a hotel-keeper. He talks of his 'establishment' with pride. He's mixed up in all sorts of dodgy deals.

When he kicked Valente out, we all refused to pay our daily rent. He said he'd call the police. We told him the cops would be more than happy to stick their noses in his business and inspect the showers and his books. Then he turned the heating off. It was January. After three days, we started paying again. We never saw Valente again. He wanted to go back to Brazil.

∽

I wash with a mini soap. I like feeling the roughness of my skin, the way it goes taut and chapped after washing. Shower gel's too gentle. It leaves your skin slightly greasy, like when you oil it. I prefer it when my skin's dry. I feel cleansed – disinfected. I soap my face too. I frown. My skin feels tight – I like that sensation. I've got little zits on my neck, apparently it's the rubbing because I always wear a scarf. Not acne or blackheads, but dry little zits. I scratch them and scrape them off with my nails. Sometimes, there's one that won't come off, so I save it until the next day. When I go back to my room after my shower, that's my little task.

After that, I'm hungry. I boil an egg or heat up a tin of food. I breakfast in front of the TV. It's a load of rubbish, but I like watching it.

∽

I'm a streetwalker. Not a call girl or anything like

that, no, a common streetwalker with high heels and menthol cigarettes.

∽

This morning, I'm going somewhere to do someone a big favour. I don't intend to go into detail and tell you about my childhood, my love life and all my woes. I'm not going to tell you how I ended up like this – you'd get too much of a kick out of it. All you're going to get is my day. If you were expecting me to talk about rape, being abandoned, HIV and heroin, you can fuck off, pervert. You'll get nothing more than my day, which is just like all the other days of my life and just like all the days to come until I die. There'll be no family tragedy, front-page news or armchair psychology.

∽

It's a nice day – not that it makes any difference to me. I walk in the shade. I'm wearing a trenchcoat, and I look like a typist, even though I'm not going to the office. Under my trenchcoat, latex. I like that word. *Latex*. It smacks in your mouth.

I wait for the bus, smoking a fag. The 21 to Glacière Arago.

I listen to the sounds of the city as if it's music. A folk song with people walking and children playing.

⌇

I like jailbirds. They're sweet! They want to marry me. They don't have any other options. I refuse to play the tart with a heart who *likes* giving pleasure, but for the guys in Santé prison, it's different. It's less sad. It's less sad because it's sadder.

⌇

I write in the bus. Schoolkids are on their way to lunch. The old people go about their old people's business. They know all the stops, they know all the streets. I'd like to know what they're thinking about inside their little old people's heads. They chew over their memories, they gnaw at them inside their tired brains. They clutch their tickets in their trembling hands. They're afraid – you can see it in their glassy little eyes. They play their part of old people.

Dominic

1

They were out to kill him. He didn't know exactly who, he didn't know exactly when, but he did know it was coming, that one of them – Father, Mother, the maid, the neighbour or Aurélie – would shove his head in the piano and crush his cheeks between the keys and the wooden lid. That's definitely how they were going to do it. They were going to crush his head in the piano in the living room.

Dominic didn't know much, but of that he was certain. The keyboard would be splattered with bits of his brain. The blood would spurt on to the wooden floor. At his funeral they'd play a Purcell march on the evil piano. The maid would have cleaned the keyboard thoroughly and flushed the bits of his brain down the toilet to avoid blocking the kitchen sink. He wouldn't even have had the privilege of the waste disposal unit. His encephalon would have vanished down the toilet like a big, cumbersome turd.

Now it was floating in the septic tank, the

keyboard had been cleaned, white as snow, his sister Aurélie was learning to play on it. The family no longer thought about little Dominic; he'd been expelled from their minds the way shit comes out of our arses and is sucked into the septic tank.

~

Dominic's childhood was kind of sad. He notched up each day as a little victory, but his anxieties soon came back to torment him. Perhaps they'd kill him tomorrow. It was a crime novel in the making. They behaved as if they loved him, as if their son were the most important thing in the world to them. But Dominic was no fool. He knew very well that beneath the veneer of the ideal family lurked a big monster full of hatred.

Since he didn't go to school, a private tutor came to the house three times a week. His name was Joncourt and he had a moustache. He carted all sorts of books around in his briefcase – algebra, geography, hundreds of typed pages, in French, in Latin and in figures.

Joncourt wasn't much fun, but at least he wasn't out to kill him. You could trust him – he wore glasses. Father wore glasses too, but it was a trap, a disguise, to gain his son's trust, a clown's mask on a villain's face.

OSCAR COOP-PHANE

Don't ask Dominic why they wanted to kill him. He had no idea. He could have done without it. It's not pleasant living in fear, with the expectation of being murdered.

This situation wasn't his choice, but here he was, in this evil family bent on crushing his head in the piano in the living room. If he'd said anything, they'd have thought he was mad. Aurélie seemed so sweet, so studious. As for his parents, they were the image of propriety, their place in heaven guaranteed. But they were out to get him and Dominic couldn't forget it. That was his only certainty, a very sad certainty.

∽

He prepared himself for it. He wrote notes explaining the circumstances of his death and hid them alongside the footpaths in the hope that one day an eager hiker would avenge him, savagely mowing down the murderous family with an axe or a machine gun. Justice would be done; there must be a God for that. The murder of a child cannot go unpunished; Joncourt's moral philosophy teachings would confirm that, no question. Only evil people like Father, Mother, the maid, the neighbour and Aurélie would wish the opposite.

∽ 10 ∽

Oh, they were very cruel beneath their pretence of being the perfect family! Killing their own son, their own flesh and blood, by jamming his head in a piano! A heinous crime, yes, it would be a heinous crime. Compared with them – with what they were planning to do sooner or later – Pierre Rivière, that guy in the nineteenth century who hacked his family to death, was a model of respectability. There was nothing worse than what they were going to do. If Dominic were able to rely on an epidemic, a war or an earthquake, he might have a hope of surviving, of not ending up with bits of his brain floating around in the toilet bowl, floating in the septic tank like a common turd. Only the deaths of Father, Mother, the maid, the neighbour and Aurélie could free him from his tragic destiny, save his life, keep his head intact – yes, only all their deaths. If he ran away, they'd be bound to catch him and drag him back to the house by the scruff of his neck, to the piano, the torture instrument on which his very last tears would fall. A few drops would plop on to the shiny keys, his final ordeal. Bang, suddenly, the lid strikes his head. Once, twice, three times, until his skull explodes like a watermelon, until his brains are splattered all over the walls.

They'd have a good laugh, Father, Mother,

the maid, the neighbour and Aurélie. They'd all laugh in unison, then they'd link hands and dance around Dominic's lifeless little body, pale and thin, his head crushed, unrecognizable.

He could just picture the little party they'd have over his corpse, the morbid celebration they'd long been anticipating.

～

It was very cowardly of them. Dominic was only twelve, unable to defend himself. What had he done to deserve such a fate? Nothing, strictly speaking, he'd done nothing wrong. He had been born, and as soon as he was old enough to grasp the fact, he knew in his heart that one day they'd kill him with that evil piano.

He must be imagining it. Sometimes he tried to convince himself he was, but to no avail; he felt it in his bones as being the only certainty he had ever had. It was his intuition speaking. It was an obvious fact. They were going to kill him. He even knew how they were planning to do it.

2

No one has ever understood him. They'd locked him up decades ago for his own safety. Now, he's protected within these four walls. Here at least no one will kill him. Only a bit of dealing, the occasional rape. But that doesn't bother Dominic. It's not packs of cigarettes or anal sex that'll make him regret what he did. It was self-defence, their deaths were his only way out. And if people can't understand, then that's their problem. The judges, the screws, opinion – public opinion, that is – he's not bothered. Here, he's at peace. He has his room, they bring him food, he can borrow books from the library. If he's well behaved, he can even watch television. Here, he's free; no one's going to kill him. No, truly, he feels no remorse. He'd taken his destiny into his own hands.

He's even made a friend called Georges. He doesn't talk much, but he's really cool. He and Dominic take their shower together.

Georges has saved up a bit of money. He's the one who buys the cigarettes and medicines, coffee and a bit of dope sometimes. Life's pleasant here. You don't want for anything. You have enough to eat, in winter they give you blankets. It's a bit dirty, of course, but you get used to it. No truly, Dominic has no regrets. It was that or death.

~

Today's his birthday, his forty-eighth spring as
Georges says. Dominic really doesn't like celebra-
tions. Georges promised him a surprise at lunch-
time, in the visiting room. Good old Georges,
what the hell's he got up his sleeve? He's a nice guy,
thinks Dominic. He pays for the cigarettes and
shower gel, medicines and instant coffee. And he
gives me surprises! I'm really lucky to be banged
up with him. Lucky to share his room. The guy
before wasn't half as decent. He was a thug and he
snored. Sharing a cell with him wasn't a life. But
Georges is nice. All he asks for is a little blow job
from time to time. Dominic doesn't like that, especially when it all spurts out. But hey, it's soon done
and he's happy to smoke and drink coffee for free.
Georges is a good mate, he won't let him down.

～

This morning, Georges has made some little cakes
for Dominic's birthday and has even found a
candle. Dominic's pleased, he blows on the flame;
he's going to see his forty-eighth spring.

'They were trying to kill me. That's why I'm here. I promise you I'm not bad. They were out to kill me. I had no choice.'

'I know, sweetheart. Tell me, was it Georges who sent you?'

'Yes, it's for my birthday. Forty-eight springs, as he says.'

'What a lovely present Georges has given you.'

'I don't know. I don't know how to do it. I've never been able to.'

'Don't worry, I'll show you. We've got twenty minutes. Now try and relax a little.'

'OK, lady.'

⁓

Good old Georges! You never know what he'll come up with next. But this is a first. Dominic, poor Dominic. Really sad, really hard done by. And completely bonkers to boot.

On the bus home. Can they imagine what I've just done? I doubt it. What about them, what have they been up to? Actually, I don't give a shit. I don't need them. I don't care what happens to them, they don't exist for me. We're on the same bus. They don't speak and neither do I.

∽

I have no compassion, that's something I've lost. I don't even feel anything for the kids in the street, the cute little creatures with blond or dark curls throwing sticks and running around all over the place. I'm surrounded by jelly, it feels as if I'm flailing around at the bottom of a big jar of jam. It sticks to my skin. I can't shake it off. I'm in this jar, with my cheeks stuck to a high glass wall. I press my forehead against it and wait my turn for the knife to come and then squidge me on the burning-hot toast. Sickly sweet goo that sticks to your skin. I've lost my compassion. It'll never come back now, I'm too old.

∽

If only I were truly alone. Don't count on it. We're alone in the midst of people, we're alone in the midst of their solitude, we're alone with others. People stink, swarm and sweat. I don't run away from them, but I don't go near them either.

They're simply there, as alone as I am. I used to think that men paid me to get away from all that. Perhaps that's what they think too. But I can tell you that when they screw me, when they get all horny jiggling about on top of my poor inert body, those sad suckers are well and truly alone. We don't share anything. They're alone when they fuck me. They're faced with nothing but a waiting body, an absent body, its mind elsewhere, a body that's simply trying not to feel too much pain. They can't be unaware of it, they can't forget that they're alone when they're with me. Guys think they come to talk to me, that they're unhappy, that I help them. I give them nothing but the harshest image of their lives, the reflection of their misery. That's all they get. Bankers, family men, workers, guys with syphilis, poets, boxers, they all wallow in the same swamp. They leave more dejected than when they arrived. You can see it in their faces, their features puffy with loneliness – that bitch solitude, which they can't do anything about. Go on, try, get married, fuck old whores, have kids, read novels, you'll always be alone. Christ, it's about time you accepted that that's your destiny. It's bitter, but you still have to swallow it.

I'm going to sleep for a bit, so I don't have to think about my life.

∽

I don't know why I write. It churns me up, it soils me from inside. Honestly, I don't know why I'm doing this. To pass the time, perhaps. That's it. I write like some people do crosswords, it keeps me busy. I think about words, style, the shapes of the letters. I feel as if I'm doing something without getting up off my arse. It's not vital, it's not therapeutic. I don't know, I write to keep my hands occupied, like doodling on Post-its when you're on the phone. I fill pages, writing one sentence after another. It's a pointless exercise, but it keeps me busy. I could listen to the radio, do sudokus, read the paper or look out of the window, but I write, I don't know why. I kill time. It's a tough bastard.

I'm a pen-pushing old slag. How about that?

∽

I'm not a fanatic. I don't like literary types. I don't like those guys with greasy hair who smell of the second-hand bookstalls on the banks of the Seine. I don't like the hairy students who take the métro to go to the library. I can't stomach their accent. They turn me off much more that those evil Le Pen supporters in the north who admire that smarmy newsreader Jean-Pierre Pernaut.

They think clever thoughts. They talk of Zola and Montesquieu. I spew my ignorant guts in their faces.

I tend to let my hate run away with me when I write. I should stop it. I don't really mean it. I don't loathe people as much as I make out. It's easier to hate, to write that you puke over all those arseholes, that you cheerfully shit on them. You feel alive, you feel above all that. To be honest, I'm no better than they are. I can't bring myself to hate them.

⌇

I could write about my squeaking window, about my aching feet. Not now. Writing makes me anxious. I don't know how to go about it. I'm afraid to talk about myself. I smoke a cigarette, feeling wistful. Maybe that's enough. A chair, a cigarette and a vacant look. I don't know. I can't think of anything special enough to write about. I feel hollow – as commonplace as a chamber pot that you plonk down beside a bed. An old pot full of spunk who hangs around the Gare Saint-Lazare and comes home to the Zenith Hotel in the middle of the night to try and think about nothing and sleep. I wish I was able to not give a fuck, to live as I please, in a cave, drinking cool water. I'm not brave enough.

I've got no nerve. Maybe one day I'll develop

some. And I'll follow it outside my body, wherever it leads me. What else can I do but wait? I harbour my little woes, caress my little scorchmarks. I don't try and heal them. I wait for them to leave my flesh. You live with your burns. What else can you do?

We can recall what we were two months or a year ago. No need to go very far back to be a stranger to oneself.

⌐

Good old Nanou who sucks and fucks. And who suffers, like everyone else, in silence, without really knowing why.

I've seen some things in my time, believe you me.

I find it all so absurd that I just try and get by as best I can.

I don't like my life, but I wouldn't want to live anyone else's life. I find other lives even more sickening than my own, which isn't much fun. We live as we do, we'd never cope with life otherwise. I'm a prostitute for all eternity.

Emmanuel

Emmanuel has blue eyes. Right now, they're wide open. It's very late, but Emmanuel hasn't closed them. His wife's asleep next to him. She's fat. Emmanuel loves her anyway, he doesn't mind that she's fat. And besides, he can play with her breasts – pretend to lose himself in them. Her name is Estelle and she snores gently. Not loudly, just a deep breath in that can't find its way out of her stomach, obstructed by fat. At first, it used to irritate him, but he's gradually grown used to it.

You get used to the things life throws at you – Emmanuel grasped that a long time ago. There's Estelle sleeping next to him; she snores a bit, she's fat. You get used to it. This is my life now. She's the one who irons my shirts and cooks. Sometimes she nags a bit, but it never lasts long. And anyway, I must be sympathetic – her job makes her anxious. Emmanuel does the same job. He's a high-school supervisor. He supervises all day long. He has responsibilities. At all hours, you have to go to the upper floors and lock the classrooms. Before turning the key, you make sure there's no one left in the room. You have an early lunch, and while the kids are having theirs, you patrol the playground. You pick up the yellow sponge balls, you go sniffing round the toilets to see if there's a smell of cigarette smoke. You stand there bolt upright by the door, your hands behind your back dangling a big bunch of keys. And then you have to collect all the pink and blue forms and log all the absentees and latecomers on the office computer. You mustn't make any mistakes: it goes down on their reports. Those things are important, otherwise you can get students into trouble unfairly. You phone their parents at an inconvenient moment, when it's not their fault. They work, too; they can't keep track of their kids all the time. But if the kids don't show up, you have to inform them. You call them, you apologize for disturbing them, you explain that little Jérôme hasn't come to school this morning, so that they know, so they don't worry. And they thank you. You tell them you have to fill in a little pink form explaining why. You thank them and say have a nice day.

∽

Yesterday was hard work. Before the holidays, it's always the same. The kids don't want to be in school. It's all very well yelling at them and punishing them, those wretched brats are oblivious. And some of them are just plain stupid. You do everything you can for them, you stop them cheating or drinking in secret, and all you get is spitting and abuse. They give you a nickname and they take the piss behind your back. You try to do everything right, to keep to the rules and teach them to do the same. They don't want to know, they only think of themselves. They let off bangers and water bombs, they throw paper pellets at your back. Some of them have weapons, Biro pea-shooters and rubber bands stretched between the thumb and index finger. They're rich kids, it's a private school.

It's the same routine, day in and day out. There are the public holidays, but they're all in May. Every day it's the same old, same old. You have to be there a quarter of an hour before the students, that's a responsibility. 8.15. And Estelle wants space, so we live in the suburbs. We don't use the car in the week, the train's more practical. There's one at 7.12. Has to be that one. The next one, the 7.45, gets there too late. A twenty-minute journey.

First compartment, third door from the end. It's by the métro exit. You see the same people in the compartment in the morning. Sometimes there's one who's not a regular and he takes your seat. You can't hold it against him, he doesn't realize. Still, it's annoying. But that's life. You go because you have to. Often, it's crowded – you're all crammed together, people step on each other's toes. Everyone's on their way to work.

There are hundreds like us. We simply don't see them. Actually, it's a bit scary, it sort of hits you in the stomach, like when you realize you're going to die.

When I have the time to think about it, that is. Otherwise I have to deal with the absences or Estelle. It all takes time, keeps my mind busy. I don't look at the other people, I think about my own business. And besides, I've got Estelle and the family, that's plenty.

∽

Emmanuel's father used to be in the military. He's retired now. He's been places and done things! He was in Sudan. Darfur. He drove tanks and jumped with a parachute. He fired a submachine gun; he peeled spuds. Emmanuel's father was a hero, and

Emmanuel has always been fascinated by him. Sometimes he talks to his colleagues about his father, but they don't understand. His father is better at recounting his exploits. Emmanuel struggles to find the words. He's slower, like a guy who's no good at telling jokes. It's all there in his head, but he can't get the words out. He's aware of it when he talks. But he can't help it, sometimes he gets the urge to talk about his father.

There are dark circles beneath his blue eyes. Administrative, industrious circles, not tiredness from partying or drinking. What's making Emmanuel tired is his life. It troubles him and he can't sleep.

No one notices his nose. His chin juts out a bit. He has a goatee, trimmed around his mouth. His wife says it makes him look dapper, and it doesn't take long to do. He's never known how to dress. Now, it's Estelle who chooses his clothes. A nice shirt and smart trousers. He looks good in shirts – he doesn't look slovenly. You have to keep up appearances in front of the students. You have responsibilities, and they judge you on what they see, they don't look beyond. If you're slovenly, they get ideas straight away, and after that they have you at their mercy. They find the crack, they pour into it like little black ants and eat you alive. You have to show them who's boss. They're not there for amusement either.

～

Emmanuel doesn't like children. Estelle though, she wants one. It's scary. A kid messes up everything. We'd have to rethink our lives when we are fine just as we are. You spend years trying to get a decent job, you know how it all works and what you have to do. A kid turns everything upside down, it knocks down all the cards you've stacked up, like a big gust of wind.

That's Estelle for you. We're settled, we've got ourselves sorted out. The minute things are going smoothly, as they should be, and we could just relax, she has to rock the boat. We'd have to rebuild everything around us. Months of preparation so that everything fits together nicely and we wouldn't even get to enjoy it. That's what a child would do, we'd have to rethink everything, the apartment for example. And if we move, that means changing our schedule, taking a different train, a different compartment and a different door, without even knowing where the métro exit is.

With a kid, you're venturing into the unknown. You can't go to the cinema on Saturday night like you did before. What do you do on Saturday night with a kid? And we don't get enough sleep as it is. If we're going to have broken nights as well … no, that's no life. Estelle, sweetheart, we'll see later, we're fine as we are, just the two of us. We like our jobs. We go to the cinema on Saturday night. And besides, with your dickey heart it's not a good idea. And he thinks about how much weight she'd put on. Perhaps a baby in her tummy wouldn't show. But he doesn't say that to her. He's right, that wouldn't go down well. He doesn't say it, but he chuckles when he thinks about it. Mustn't laugh in front of her. To stop himself, Emmanuel pinches his thigh through his trouser pocket. When Estelle's upset, it's best not to wind her up. Otherwise things go awry and he can't touch her for a month. She bears grudges, she never forgets. Emmanuel would like to make all the decisions, but Estelle is stronger.

Sometimes, you have to give in – Father often says so. He knows what he's talking about, he's seen his share of enemies. Not minor domestics in the suburbs, but gun battles ending in death. He's got loads of friends who died. One of them had both his legs cut off above the knee. When Emmanuel was little, it gave him the creeps. Mind how you go, son, or you'll end up like Gillou. After that he could no longer blithely ride his bike, he was haunted by the image of Gillou, who'd stepped on a mine. No legs, no bike. And the two pink stumps sticking out of Gillou's shorts were ugly. Despite that, he seemed happy, he was always telling jokes. And then one day, he blew his brains out. Bang! They said he was cleaning his gun, but Emmanuel wasn't fooled, he'd seen it on TV, they say he was cleaning his gun so the widow can get the pension. A funeral with full honours for Gillou. Even though he had no legs, the coffin was the normal size.

A gun salute and red-white-and-blue flags. Flowers everywhere. Father had got out his uniform. He keeps it in the big cupboard in the sitting room. When Emmanuel was little, he used to touch all the badges stuck on like buttons. With the tip of his index finger. Had to be careful, the uniform was kept in a polythene cover. Like at the dry cleaners. Father didn't want him to touch it, had to be careful.

The real medals were in the display case. A glass tower kept locked. His mother cleaned it every Sunday. Emmanuel had never managed to open it, he'd never found out where the guns were. Now he could ask Father but he was a bit ashamed. And what would he do with guns? They're dangerous, believe me.

The train pulls into the station. Emmanuel gets off. Now he has to take the métro. Not the same atmosphere. You feel more rushed. It's not unpleasant, you're stepping into your day. It's hard to get a seat. If you're lucky, you can grab one of the folding seats, but the standing passengers press against them.

Emmanuel picks up his newspaper in the métro. The headlines, the pretty photos, a horoscope and a crossword. All that he gets free. It's something to read at work.

Today, there's too much to do. He went to Barcelona with the Year Elevens and the absence slips have piled up. You go away for four days, you come back, and you have to catch up.

Emmanuel is all on his own with his absence slips. The others don't help him: recording the absentees is his job. And annoyingly, when he talks to Estelle about it, she doesn't hear a thing. She chops her vegetables and gives little grunts to give the impression she's listening. So, Emmanuel is all on his own with his absence slips. Pink forms, blue forms. They have to be sorted, filed, recorded. The absences go down on the students' reports. The parents have to explain them. It's a lot of work, and that's a fact.

Emmanuel likes doing the absences but it's not very rewarding. No one ever talks to him about it except when things go wrong. And then it surges back like a huge wave. That's why Emmanuel says it's a long-term job, like taking on the sea. He was the one who'd asked for these responsibilities, so now he can't complain. Sometimes he could do with a helping hand. The other supervisors have different tasks. They can't understand what's involved. They collect the students' forms, bung them in the in-tray and *basta*, they go off for a little wander, the bastards. They're forever going outside for a smoke and they're always laughing. Emmanuel doesn't smoke. He's convinced the others make fun of him. He can tell when sometimes he walks into the office, the others are falling around laughing and suddenly they stop. He's tried talking to them but he gets a strong feeling that they don't like him. Anyway, we're there to do our job! Yes, but all the same, it would be nice to have some friends at work. It would take his mind off things, it would be less stressful. Still the same responsibilities but they'd help out, like Father in the war. If he'd had to rely only on himself, Father would have died – he often says so. All in the same boat. Each person at their post, ready to help their mates if there's a hitch. Mustn't go under, if one goes, we all go. You feel supported, invincible. But Emmanuel is well and truly on his own with his absence slips.

∽

In any case, in life you're always alone, he reckons. You're alone with your wife, you're alone with your friends. No point going around wiggling your arse, it might turn people on but at the end of the day, you're the one who's steering the ship. However much you depend on them, have a little laugh and delegate a bit, you're alone. Now that he's grasped that, he's more relaxed. You walk through rooms, the office, the métro, the car park; you're alone, you pass through and you move on. Actually it's not unpleasant. You know who you can count on. You fight. It's a jungle. Sometimes you win. That's how Emmanuel has chosen to see things. On the whole, life's going well. You have to earn your bread and butter to have a bit of comfort. He'd found a good job and settled down with Estelle. She's fat, but you can't have it all. And anyway, Emmanuel has never thought of himself as particularly attractive. Not an ugly mug either, but he's certain that people don't notice him. At school he had a friend who said he didn't stand out against a white wall. In a way, that's how Emmanuel thinks of his face.

He's no pin-up, for sure, just a regular guy. But he's honest, and that's what matters. Estelle says that honest men are few and far between. All the others think about is getting you between the sheets! She sounds as if she's talking from experience, but Emmanuel's pretty certain that it's never happened to her – she reads women's magazines.

⌒

Estelle does the same job as Emmanuel but she doesn't like it. She can't stand a single one of the kids. Emmanuel feels more torn. He talks to them. Not all of them, but the nice ones, he asks how they are, tells them jokes. He tells himself that the students will remember him. You have to get the balance right. Not too keen, not too mean. When he started the job, one of the teachers told him to be merciless at the start of the year. It sets the boundaries, he said. You can cut them some slack later on. That's the way it is, there are rules. You can't just do as you like.

Now, he's beginning to understand, but it wasn't easy at first. It's a real profession. When he first started the job, he wanted out. And then, little by little, he told himself that everything was fine and he stayed. He signed a permanent contract.

Initially, he wanted to be a teacher. History and Geography. You need a diploma. He sat the teaching exam three times. They're not easy, those things. This year, he didn't attempt it. He told himself that after all, he had everything he needed. Later, he might be promoted to senior supervisor, maybe, and anyway, Emmanuel has never wanted loads of money. He lacks for nothing; he and Estelle have two cars. He's never liked guys who flash their money around. The image that comes into his mind is a guy getting out of a car with a girl on each arm. The three of them look a little the worse for wear; they go to a restaurant. The girls are wearing dresses. Tits spilling out, like in the ads. The guy's wearing leather shoes. He's shorter than the girls. They shriek with laughter when he whispers something into their necks. He talks dirty and they make a great pretence of being shocked, they laugh, tossing their heads back. You can see their teeth gleaming in the dark. He takes them into the restaurant. They have to walk up some steps. They're going to carry on drinking, that's for sure. And then afterwards, the guy will take them to a hotel. They'll snort some coke and fuck like dogs.

When he thinks of images like that, Emmanuel's lips tend to quiver. He's not too sure what he's looking at. It perturbs him and his lips tremble a little, like at the beginning of a kiss, before it all goes mad. Sometimes he's aware of it. He likes catching himself out. In a way he feels as if he is escaping from himself, as if he were no longer in control of his body, as if he, Emmanuel Tavernier, were governed by a dark force. He's been a fan of stories of dark forces ever since he was very little. Trolls and magic rings. On his bookshelves, there's nothing but fat books with American covers. A big title, the author's name in big letters, all embossed. He finds them at Saint-Michel. When Emmanuel reads a book, he loses himself in it. He reads all the time, when he's walking and in the corridors of the métro. That's what he loves, entering into another world. Estelle says it's his need to escape. She's a woman, she always has to use psychological words. She wants to explain everything. He tries not to think about it, otherwise he gets anxious. She comes out with stuff like that when they're eating in front of the TV and it makes him panicky. He comforts himself by saying she's a woman, she has to explain everything, or she wouldn't be able to cope. But when he thinks about things like that, it's as if the light around him were changing. It turns greyish; it runs down the walls. He doesn't like those moments when it feels as though everything is flying away. He forgets his responsibilities, the absences and paid holidays, the office chair and the train timetable. When she starts explaining, Estelle's words turn his little admin system upside down. He's never spoken about it, but now he's beginning to know himself; he can tell when the light is about to change. He's not sure whether other people experience the same thing. He doesn't know whether like him they sometimes feel sad for no reason. It's not like when something happens to you, it's stranger than that. You feel it in your body, you feel a bit dizzy. Eventually it passes and you go back to what you were doing.

~

He indulges in moments of relaxation, TV in the evenings, when he's tired. After being on your feet all day long, on the lookout, it's nice to be able to come home and unwind. When Estelle hasn't got her period and is in a good mood, things can get a bit wild. Emmanuel loves sex. He feels a bit

ashamed afterwards but he feels free. It's not like in
the films, though. It's never like in the films.

What Emmanuel likes best is breasts. He finds
big breasts comforting. When he was little, he
stared at breasts the whole time. Now he tries to be
more discreet. Just a glance to size them up without
looking at the girl, and he thinks about them again
afterwards. In the street or in the métro, he fixes
an image of boobs in his mind like a photo and
thinks about them again, staring vacantly, sometimes for hours. When he has sex with Estelle, he
thinks about other girls he's seen, about all the
ones he'll never have, tall and short, brunettes and
redheads, the girl in the bakery. There are so many.
He doesn't think about seducing them. Shadows.
He fixes the image firmly in his mind and that way
he can think about it whenever he wants.

∽

On Sundays, Estelle goes to see her mother. He
stays at home.

It's become a habit. He goes into the sitting
room and draws the curtains, then he takes off his
clothes and sits on the sofa. That's when it all begins
properly. At first, he rubs his belly with the palm of
his hand. He continues like that for five minutes,

thinking about a girl he's seen. He always has a little rag beside him. What would Estelle say if she found a stain on the sofa! Best not to think about it.

Then he twists round and rubs himself against the sofa arm. Like Granny's dog against visitors' legs. Sharp little thrusts. Convulsive, his naked body racked with tremors, his back to the coffee table. His legs are straight, paralysed, his feet on the floor, his hunched body espousing the curves of the armrest. He rubs himself again. When he feels he's about to come, he stands upright on the sofa cushions and finishes the job by hand. He grabs his penis with both hands, pumping hard. His feet dig into the deep foam cushions. Hundreds of images flood into his mind. Bodies banging into each other. A crowd of bodies. And he rubs against them all as if trying to get inside them. He dominates. The girl from the bakery is always there. Her face stands out. She smiles at him. Emmanuel loves that.

When it's over, he wipes everything, puts his clothes back on, opens the curtains and sits on the sofa re-living it all, waiting for Estelle. He finds the images that go through his mind at those times a bit smutty, but that's what he likes and anyway, he's not doing anyone any harm. Other people must do the same.

Sometimes, when he's sitting on the sofa with Estelle, he thinks about it. It makes him laugh a little. Right there, where the two of them are watching TV! Honestly! He's a bit ashamed and he stops thinking about it. He stares at Estelle's big breasts and goes back to watching TV.

The living room is not very big but it's got all mod cons. A sofa, a TV. They've even put in a little bar with lots of different bottles on it. It's for when they entertain. Which is rare. Estelle says she doesn't enjoy herself because she's in and out of the kitchen. And anyway, five people eating around a coffee table isn't practical. They eat out, it's more convenient.

There's a little Italian on the main road. Emmanuel and Estelle have dinner there sometimes. The two of them, gazing into each other's eyes. He always has lasagne, which irritates Estelle. He never has anything different – the lasagne's good, he doesn't see why he should have something different. They know them there, him and Estelle. The waiter looks like a real Eyetie. His name's Édouard. Estelle always wants to leave him a tip. She always says he's stylish. Sometimes, Emmanuel's jealous. At the same time, he likes it. It's simple, whenever they come home from the restaurant, Estelle wants to do stuff. It never failed. Driving home, he gets himself in the mood. He chooses the girls he's going to think about. He's happy, he feels as if he's earned his treat. It's never especially passionate, but it's worth it anyway.

Then they go to sleep. It's a school day tomorrow.

'Call me Nanou.'

'OK, Nanou. I don't normally do this, you know. I'm a school supervisor. I've got responsibilities.'

'Stop talking, will you. Do you like my breasts?'

'Yes, they're big.'

'Do you want to play with them?'

'Yes, can I rub myself against them?'

It's worse when it's cold. I see the customer coming (I wish there was another word, I'm not running a business), we're going to be in the warm. I swallow my pride for some dosh and ten minutes' electric heating.

~

I'm not in good health, I stink of the street. I'm a girl who's spent her whole life doing this, who doesn't know how to do anything else. I think that's what they want. It's OK to despise me. It makes them feel civilized, it gives them a sense of power. They get turned on by an old trollop who reeks of syphilis and mulled wine. They find it comforting to taste destitution, to defile themselves a little. When they get home, they'll have a shower and forget all about it.

I wash myself too, but it doesn't come out. Their filth is under my skin, under my nails, in my hair. Their smell clings to my body. I scrub myself raw but I can't get rid of it. Even though I've been doing this for a long time, you don't get used to other people's filth. It contaminates you as much as it did on the first day.

~

These are not the days of cheerful brothels and soldiers on leave. The guys don't boast about it. There's nothing clever about damaging me a little more. I can tell from their body language that they despise me. That's my only contact with men. It's quite something.

Selling my body and my cunt, my mouth and my hands is a freedom that I give myself. It never lasts long, five or six minutes at most. The rest is chit-chat, answering their questions, laughing at their jokes – that's another form of prostitution.

∽

Every morning I loathe myself a little bit more. It's all very well telling myself that I don't have to get up at 5 a.m. and jump on a commuter train, put on white clogs Crocs and serve frozen meals in a works canteen, it's all very well telling myself that I have my freedom, I don't have to work nine-to-five or file tax returns or fend off a lecherous boss, I still loathe myself.

There's no going back. You're a prostitute for life. The ones who give it up will always remain whores. You're branded, a tattoo on the heart.

∽

The street is the world I know. It doesn't make me feel good. Sometimes, I long for the countryside, farmers and cornfields. Work the land, the green belt. Rise with the sun and go to bed at nightfall, after a bowl of nice, rich broth.

But there too, it's the same misery. The man of the fields, his bestiality, his talk ... we've known and hated each other for generations.

In Paris, at least, you can count on anonymity. Being lost in the crowd without anyone bothering. There are swarms of people all around your body, but no one notices you.

Victor & Baton

Baton is sixteen years old. He's going to die. He's weak, he doesn't want to go out any more. He's already had operations on his eyes, his mouth and his heart. He drags himself about, he shits on the floor. Victor's afraid of ending up on his own.

This morning, Baton wouldn't allow Victor to wash him. He thrashed about under the shower head, letting out little yelps of pain and scratching the enamel on the bath. Victor could no longer bear to see him suffering; he carried him like a child and put him on his bed.

Baton eats very little, he no longer wants to drink. Dr Blanchet says there's nothing more to be done. Baton is sixteen years old, he's going to die. Science can't prevent it. Victor has a taste of rage in his mouth, an acid taste that won't go away. He is as powerless as science and Dr Blanchet.

He must make Baton's life as comfortable as possible before he dies, take him out for a little walk from time to time. Baton needs to smell the world before leaving it. He can't see colours, so smell is important to him. Baton was abandoned at birth.

Victor took him in and washed him, caring for him like his own son. He raised him in his little apartment in the 11th *arrondissement*. He made him a space in the sitting room, in his life, in his heart. When he went off to work, Baton waited for him. Now Victor no longer works, he can spend more time with him, the only soul who has never deserted him. They love each other like family. In his wallet, Victor carries a photo of Baton, as he would of his son if he had one. But all the women who might have given him one had left him. That's life. He has no one but Baton, and he was about to die. Victor's woes are not over! There's still a great deal of suffering in store for him, on top of all the never-ending shit that's happened to him. And it wasn't about to stop: as long as he lives, he'll continue to be stabbed all over – in the heart, the stomach, the leg – everywhere. He'll end up lying in a pool of blood on a tiled bathroom floor, unable to get up again.

Baton must have suffered too, but Victor had rescued him. Wordlessly, they'd rescued each other. And now, Baton is dying. What will become of poor Victor? He's going to end up alone, after all these years. He might not be able to cope. But let's not think about that for the moment. Baton is here – he needs looking after. He shakes his head, sometimes he scratches himself, slowly, as if making the effort of one final gesture. Watching him, Victor feels as if fingernails are pinching his heart, the blood dripping drop by drop from his organs, like tears in his flesh. It is overflowing, poisoning him. It fills his head until it explodes. Grief-induced hydrocephalus.

He can picture Baton as if it were yesterday, running until he's left panting, his tongue hanging out, froth bubbling with life around his mouth. Baton has always had that energy, as if he were somehow flying above life. No, he's no ordinary dog, but he's sixteen, and multiplied by seven, that means he's old and is going to die.

Every story comes to an end. And this will be the end of their story.

∽

Paris too seemed to be dying that day. The cyclists, the cars, even the tarmac were breathing their last. A white veil, like a shroud, enveloped everything. You immersed yourself in your occupations. Your soles stuck to the ground, as if trying to adhere to it, to stop you from losing your footing. Baton ambled slowly – he didn't even sniff at the rivulets of piss running down the pavements. What's the point of marking your territory when you're going to die? He avoided the gaze of other dogs, moving a little closer to Victor's legs each time. Victor kept walking, hunched, resigned, for love of the dog. Perhaps they'd share their final moments? Mustn't think of it. Keep walking, eye the girls like before, impress them with his tweed jacket, show off, Baton on the leash. He and Baton would explore the parks, he'd throw sticks for Baton and they'd have a bit of fun, to escape the crushing burden of solitude. When there are two of you, it's more practical. You've got an excuse, you're taking the dog out, letting him do his thing, he needs to crap. People don't look at you the way they do when you're on your own. He's taking his dog for a walk, it's perfectly normal, it's midnight, he must have a wife waiting for him at home watching TV. A dog gives you an excuse to live as you please, going out in the middle of the night so as not to be stuck at home. It makes you look composed, it stops people trampling on you with their dirty looks.

Victor chewed all that over in his mind. It's calming to keep turning over old thoughts. It soothes your anxiety, you have the feeling that nothing's changed, that Baton's not going to die and that you're walking as usual, the two of you, around République. This little ritual filled Victor with happiness. Women he'd written off a long time ago. They're all the same, only good for sucking your money out of you like marrow and then running off with a sailing instructor once the bone's sucked dry. They were very cruel and very predictable. All he needed was the occasional bit of flesh, a nice blow job so he could go to sleep with a smile on his face. You get by on your own, you make up stories – you squeeze the juice with the right hand, for health reasons, to make yourself feel a bit better. It's more practical – women give you grief, they call the tune, they make you do things you'd never have imagined. When all's said and done, you end up on your own anyway. They say it's because you drink too much, because you don't pay them enough attention, but from the start, they knew they'd be leaving once there was nothing left to take. That's what they're like, they suck you to put you to sleep, thought Victor. And then they take everything from you, your pride with it. They discard you, like a donkey. Women, vipers, men, traitors or arseholes. There's no one but Baton.

But you can't escape humanity. It's always there, like a gaping wound that will never heal. It sweats, it drips. Sir, you're going to lose your leg. It's gangrenous, it's eating your bones. You scratch the pus along your shin. You'll see, it won't be easy. You have to watch out, it won't go away. You have to live with it – try to get rid of it and you'll starve to death. It's your fate. It's sad, the only way out is to die.

Victor isn't bitter, he's just resigned. He wanted too much, he wasn't given enough. The game's over, he's retiring. He won't outlive his dog. What does it matter, he's done his time, he's seen what he wanted to see, he's tasted joys and sorrows. Baton's time has come, his too, it's no big deal. They'll go to sleep together, it will be beautiful, it will be simple. Farewell, sorrow.

∽

There isn't much in Victor's apartment. He's never liked furniture. Just loads of leaflets piled up as if they were necessary. He doesn't know why he keeps them, he just does it out of habit.

Victor eats little – rice, pasta and beer. He has a routine that developed naturally, a soup plate for him and a little bowl for Baton. He sits reading the newspaper. The bit he likes best is the news in brief. It's comforting to read about others' misfortunes – women kept prisoner in basements, men having sex with little boys. When he thinks about it, Victor can't see why he finds it so fascinating, but he can't resist – blood, tears, rice and beer. They're not ordinary stories, they turn your stomach, they make your gut churn like a fiery curry. Rapes, murders, horrors of all kinds, a baby eaten by rats – that's what he likes to see going on in the world. A nameless brutality that sets his heart pounding as opposed to being pounded. For a while, he is outside himself, he purifies himself from within with other people's shit. It cleanses him like a thorough wash, all that barbarism splurged in fresh ink across the headlines.

But this evening, he's unable to read, his mind is completely taken up by Baton. He keeps going back to him, he can't help it. Slumped quietly on the sofa, he doesn't watch TV; he wants no distractions. He'd like to chase away his gloomy thoughts. Why not put an end to it now, to save time? In the bathroom, reach for the barbiturates. Just for a laugh, put an end to it. It would be so easy, crush some in Baton's bowl, swallow the rest and fall asleep lying on the floor, the two of them.

He contemplates it. The moment passes. He dozes off. We'll see tomorrow.

～

Before, the dog used to sleep in his basket, but for the last few days he's been resting in Victor's bed. They fall asleep snuggled up together. They're tired after their evening walk and they drop off at once. At nights, the dog sometimes has trouble breathing, his bronchial tubes are blocked with God-knows-what, a rather unsavoury viscous liquid. Victor soothes him as best he can, to appease his dog's anxieties. They cradle each other to get through the night. You could say that they depend on each other. Neither dominates, there is a sort of balance that sustains them. Insofar as it is possible given that one is a man and the other a dog.

Baton isn't domesticated, he's not a servant, he's simply learned to live at the man's pace and to be a companion to him in his solitude. Without each other, they'd be wiped off the map. Fate's a fine thing, thinks Victor.

Baton slept badly that night; Victor, beside him, was aware of him. Even so, they woke up very late. Victor smokes in bed. He opens his eyes, a cigarette between his lips. Inhaling the smoke makes him feel alive again, sullies him a little as soon as he wakes up. The dog rouses himself. He lays his head on Victor's stomach, his ears drooping and his eyelids caked with a yellow discharge. A new day to face.

❧

Victor washes. The dog watches him scrub his naked body with a purple flannel. Baton lies with his head on the tiled floor, soaking up the splashes like a hairy bathmat. Victor towels himself and gets dressed. The dog doesn't wash himself any more, there's no one for him to charm now, no one to look at, not even any puddles of piss to sniff. Baton no longer pokes his muzzle into things, because it died before he did.

Your body falls apart, disintegrates. And eventually it's unable to carry you.

❧

They have a bite to eat and then go out for their morning walk. All the people they meet in the streets are on their way to work. They sell their labour power to the highest bidder. Their hair is combed, their shoes polished. Victor hasn't made that kind of effort for a long time. He washes, he gets dressed, that's already plenty. Freed from the office paper chains. No more Post-it notes stuck on his head, staples in his brain or ink on his hands. No more travel card. Now he buys a ticket when he has to go somewhere. They rarely leave the neighbourhood. What's the point? asks Victor. It's true, what's the point of rushing around all the time, looking for whatever it is that's missing? The same misery as here except it's somewhere else. Women ignoring you, kids shoving you, cars beeping you. A little bit of urban misery, which-ever neighbourhood you're in, whichever side of the river. So that's enough, we'll go out as little as possible since the world's not interested in us, because it bruises us and scalds us. Only to give Baton some fresh air, let him crap on the pave-ments, which, frankly, don't deserve any better. If only he could cover them in shit! That would be a laugh, slimy green shit oozing all over the pave-ments. It would dirty their shoes, it would stick to their soles, they'd slither around in it, they'd wallow in it, they'd all be covered in shit from head to foot. They'd cut a fine figure with Baton's shit behind their ears! They'd eat it, they'd fill their lungs with it.

That's all they deserve, to choke on Baton's shit, nice and runny, totally disgusting. Flies would be glued to their skin; they'd do their job before the maggots set to work. Paris like a vast squat toilet with the Seine in the middle. All those litres and litres of Baton's runny shit flowing into the sea. It would get into the buildings, the infernal tide would seep under the doors until it reached the hallways. A vile stench clinging to the walls like the most persistent grubs. Puke too, Victor's puke, which doesn't help matters. It's tough, that vomit, the bile of a pro, thickened by years and years of suffering. Yes, that would be a glorious, magnificent revenge, the world coming to an end awash with human puke and dog shit. The tidal wave people were waiting for! Liberated by the unspeakable, the stinking poison secreted by those two, Victor and Baton, cesspools of shit, chasms of puke. Here we come, take cover! Put your boots on, pull down your visors! We're all psyched up. Just this one little pleasure and we'll leave you in peace, promise, it won't last long. Let it all out in one go and we're done. There, it's not much, we just need to expel the litres of bile from our bodies. Trust me, we've been holding them in from birth.

～

There is no tsunami. Only those two shadows whose walk is haunted by apocalyptic fantasies. They walk, as is their habit. It will be a walk like thousands of previous walks. Nothing sensational, nothing astonishing, just two shadows, the first on two feet, the second on a leash. No one notices them. They progress one step at a time, two lives in which nothing changes. They stumble more and more frequently, they roll like two little polished glass marbles on an imaginary slope. The two shadows fly over people, Victor and Baton, invisible to the world.

Another day dawns. They move forward in time the way they walk through the streets. Baton isn't dead, but he's sixteen and it won't be long.

'I've got a dog. Can he come with us?'

'You want to do things with your mutt?'

'No, I don't want to leave him in the street. He's going to die. He'll lie still. His name's Baton.'

'All right, let's go then, Baton can come too.'

When I get home, I'm going to burn all this. I don't want anyone to read it. So why write? I don't know, it's stupid.

Like pretty much everything around me. I've given up trying to figure it out. I'd rather think about my coffee, Jeannot, or the owner of the Zenith Hotel. These everyday human stories are comforting, the little snippets of gossip that are our salvation. You feel alive, you think about something other than the blood running through your veins. You think about what they said or what they did – it's a bit like watching an animated postcard. Life as a TV soap that offers an escape.

⤳

I will have managed to talk about myself, though, a few pages of self-indulgence. I didn't think I was capable of it.

Forgive my style and my mistakes. Don't feel sorry for me either, that's not why I'm doing this. Like I already said, I write to kill time, so don't go thinking it's for sentimental reasons or anything like that.

⤳

I love the colour of the tarmac when it rains. The pavements sparkle as if they'd been mopped clean. If it weren't for the muddy puddles and the dirty cracks, you really might think that the ground you're walking on, the pavement where I wait and work, was radiating something new. As if we were the first people ever to walk on it. Urban adventurers, we could scratch our initials on it with a penknife. It won't graze you if you stumble. It's as smooth and slippery as an imitation-leather banquette.

I drop my cigarette butts on the pavement. I dirty it. When the lighted end lands on the ground it makes a pretty sound, *psschit*. The tobacco goes soggy, the lighted end gives up the ghost. It's no longer red, it's already black, a mixture of ash and water, like at the bottom of a plastic cup.

∽

I'm getting tired, my legs are heavy, this job consumes your body. Your soul no longer has a monopoly on suffering.

∽

I've seen everything. It would take too long to write about. And disgusting it is too.

∽

There's a guy over the street selling roses. He trails his sadness and a huge bunch of red flowers from one café terrace to another. He's looking for love, it's his bread and butter. Without those lovestruck couples, he wouldn't eat, he wouldn't be able to pay for the shabby furnished room where he stretches out his withered body. He makes his living from those who are in love. It can't be that easy when you're alone with your big red bunch of flowers. He has no one to give it to, he wants to get rid of it.

I loved someone once, but I don't want to talk about it.

⌐

I like the pages in my notebook. They're soft. I often run my palm over them before writing on them, as if I wanted them to feel my quivering heart. I can't be rough with it. I pick it up gently, so as not to hurt it.

It is an object that speaks to me.

I have a notebook and an ashtray. Nothing else matters. My electric hotplate, my cafetière, my red scarf, my aluminium toaster, all these things make my life easier, but I don't love them. My ashtray I always take with me, it's gilded and it has a little swinging lid. It's pretty.

Luc

1

They call him Moby One. His real name's Luc. He likes cigarettes, beer and mopeds. Proper ones, Motobécanes, blue, copper, red or black. He knows all the different models. Luc has made a workshop in his little ground-floor apartment. There are grease stains on the carpet, you trip over coked-up cylinder heads, but he doesn't care, it's much more convenient to take a magneto rotor flywheel to bits at home than out in the street.

For Luc, true freedom is to ride a moped until he can no longer feel his legs. He loves the wind whipping his face, the thrumming of the engine, the white fumes that follow him like his lucky star.

Luc lives with his parents. He has the ground floor. The 'rents are upstairs, on the first floor. Luc's no longer a teenager, except he's separated from his wife and he packed in his job. He started buying more and more six-packs and before he even knew it, at thirty-eight he was back living with his parents. Lucky they took him in, otherwise he'd be sleeping under a bridge or beside the railway tracks.

~

He lives on the ground floor and repairs mopeds. He's always loved tinkering with engines. He had his first bike when he was fourteen, a second-hand BB Sport. Not the one with the fuel tank under the saddle, but a real sports bike: horizontal tank, chromed cap, racing mirror, the whole caboodle. The 'rents didn't know, he kept it from them for six months. The neighbours told on him. But impudent little Luc wasn't going to be pushed around. He took to the road with his BB Sport and rode for weeks with no idea where he was going. For the first time in his life, he felt free to do what he wanted. He rode alone on the B roads, the god of the tarmac, 'FLYING BB' written in capital letters on his little full-face helmet. He had the works – the jacket and the badge. It looked good, sellotaped to his shoulder. He made up slogans. Speed king. Born to be BB Sport. He was free.

By the time he reached Orange, he was flat broke. His coil was burnt out, he had to get it sorted. Sitting by the canal – the BB Sport proudly upright on its kickstand – he sat smoking the cigarette butts he'd collected in the city centre. That's when he met Pio.

Pio was sad. He walked along the towpath with a springing step. His wife had just died. Hit by a school bus.

He offered Luc a cigarette. An English brand that wouldn't burn his lips like his lousy butts. Gestures like that go straight to the heart. Luc broke down; he cried all the tears in his body, those litres of salt water that he'd been holding in for so long.

They became friends. Pio took Luc back home, a house with stucco walls haunted by the wife he had lost.

In the little neon-lit garage, they repaired the BB. Brand new.

Pio owned an old AV 98. They decided to go on a trip together – Flying BB and Jumping AV, on the road again.

Pio dusted off his biker jacket from his youth. He dug up the little chest buried at the bottom of the garden. It contained a tidy sum, enough to keep the pair of them going for several months.

He locked up the house and they donned their helmets and jackets. They were off, full throttle, headed for Switzerland and its huge lakes.

Pio had hitched a little trailer to the back of the blue bike. It was tidier than all those bundles dangling from the rack. They had a tent made of synthetic material and tools galore. In the evenings, after riding all day, exhausted, they smoked by the fire. The pair of them made a hell of a team. Luc and Pio, Flying BB and Jumping AV, racing along the B roads at top speed.

Like true friends, they got their hands dirty, argued, repaired accelerator cables and de-coked the exhausts.

Freedom blew at their backs – it ruffled the strands of hair hanging down their necks.

～

Luc was too young to have had a wife and couldn't understand the huge grief Pio felt in the pit of his stomach. Although unable to comprehend it, he had always been smart enough to respect other people's sadness. He didn't try to feel it or sniff it, he simply bowed down before it as he would have knelt in front of a holy statue. He understood that this sadness was stronger than Pio. The main thing was to live with it, like a parasite that you feed with your own blood. It sucks at you but it's better to let it drink a few drops of blood than to chase it away and have it harrow you to the bone in retaliation. No, don't get rid of it. Live with it, go off on your moped and occasionally stroke the bitter melancholy that claws at your stomach. You have to nurture it to stop it consuming you, you have to give it the sincerest part of your being. You won't get over it, all your life there'll be this gaping wound deep in your heart. But don't worry, it won't stop beating.

⤳

The further they rode, the less Pio felt that sadness in his gut. They had to think about survival, finding food, fuel for the bikes, a place to sleep and have a wash. All these little tasks distracted him from the ghost of his departed love. On the moped, he was fleeing his wife's shadow, fleeing his sorrow, he was living, at last and in spite of everything. Jumping AV, king of the B road, invincible, more powerful than the rain, more powerful than the black ice.

But what was Luc running away from? He hadn't really suffered – apart from being bullied by Jojo Légende at school. No, Luc had no official excuse for running away. He just wanted to be free. What would he say when he went home? What would be his excuse? There are sadnesses that can't be explained.

〜

Eventually he'd have to go home, have to explain, have to go back to his boring schoolboy life – rubbish at maths, bullied by Jojo Légende, desperately in love with the pretty Mathilde Arnaud. Mathilde! He often thought about her when he was on his moped. She was so beautiful with those dark shadows under her eyes and her fair hair. One night when he couldn't sleep, sitting at his schoolboy's desk, he'd written her a poem. Four pompous verses extolling the beauties of autumn and the depth of his feelings. He'd reread it a hundred times, proud of his pen and of the melancholy lines he demanded of it. He never gave her the poem. He'd kept it hidden away under his mattress for a long time, and then one day, in a moment of sadness, he'd torn it up like a train ticket. He felt ridiculous; it made him blush to think about it when he was alone in his bedroom or in the school playground. He'd been so besotted with little Mathilde. When he was at a loose end, he thought about her. He pictured her running in her grey tracksuit, going up the school staircase or chatting to her friends. She had everything, she was pure as snow, he said so in the poem.

He thought about her less now, but sometimes her image would cloud his gaze. The road flashed past but in front of him was nothing but a pretty succession of Mathildes. One smiling, another sad or annoyed, a multitude of Mathilde Arnauds unfolding before him, replicated to infinity like reflections in a hall of mirrors. They danced, cried, shouted or swore, all those lovely Mathildes swimming before his eyes. A rose-tinted veil of mist, dazzling, sparkling, in all the sincerity of his foolishness. He couldn't force anything; his love was both that of a child and of a man, a bastard object, more poignant than anything else.

∽

They were close to the Swiss border. Lakes and tranquillity would be theirs, Fricâlin cheese and hot chocolate, watchmaking, dirty money, and all that. Switzerland had been the obvious choice. Before leaving, Pio had let that drop like a stone in a well. He had never set foot there and neither had Luc, but as long as he was on his bike, he didn't care where he went. So Switzerland it was. It would be cool, a glorious change of scene. Switzerland was nice, like a miniature country where there was no danger of getting lost. There was something comforting about it, something healthy and blooming like a roundabout. The fields, the green grass, the spring breeze. The smell of freshly washed sheets.

~

In Switzerland, they took photos with Pio's old reflex camera. One for his wife (Jeanne Robert, Plot 72d, Saint Martin cemetery, France), and the other for Luc's parents which, all things considered, was pretty dull. They hung around in Switzerland for a while, and then it was time to go home. You always end up going home, it was inescapable. The return was less thrilling.

Pio walked into his empty house, and Luc plucked up the courage to face the fossils, while dreaming of Switzerland.

2

He settled down, but he never really got mopeds out of his system. He bought T-shirts and posters. At first, it made Marine laugh being trundled around on the back of a 99Z. She said she liked it, that it reminded her of her youth. Then she fell pregnant. They lived together, and Luc had a job as a landscape gardener. Things were going well, they waited for the arrival of little Hector or little Eugénie – they didn't know the baby's sex.

Marine ended up having a miscarriage. Out of her womb came just a shrivelled embryo. It was tough for her. It was tough for him too. They both drank to forget, then came the medication and the words you suck in between your cheeks.

One morning she walked out on him. Luc found himself alone with his schnapps and his sadness. He tried to put an end to it, and failed. We know the rest, he went back to live with his parents.

He repairs mopeds and sometimes sells one to pay for beers and extras. He doesn't have a wife, only a few girls from the bar he screws occasionally. They're sales girls.

The café is just opposite Le Bon Marché. He knows them all. His mates have road-tested them too. They sell perfume and hats. On their feet all day. So in the evenings it's natural for them to sit on a stool at the bar drinking kir and smoking menthol cigarettes. There's Camille, Anna and little Margot, nicknamed Bouboule. She's a bit chubby, Bouboule, but they still like her. Always game for a quickie in the toilet. She likes doing it, she doesn't ask for anything in return. She's seen all sorts of cocks, she has. The guys from Le Babylone for starters, even the washer-upper was entitled to his blow job. The washer-upper's black, they tease him sometimes. They say it's only in fun. They laugh at his accent, they say his cock is the biggest that Bouboule has ever sucked.

Le Babylone closes at 9 p.m. But after that, the owner invites the guys and the girls to have another few drinks for the road. Luc's one of the guys, he's there every night. He looks down a little on his drinking companions, he finds them coarse. But hey, they're mates and without them he'd be very lonely in his ground-floor room every night. So he carries on going to Le Babylone, gets wasted on beer, staggers back home, alone, or with Bouboule, and falls asleep without thinking about it.

All in all, Luc's a sad guy. He repairs mopeds, he smokes beers and drinks cigarettes.

'How do I know you're not a cop?'

'How do I know you're not?'

'I've got a moped, cops don't ride around on mopeds.'

'Look at me. I'm an old prostitute.'

'OK, let's go …'

I've never had a pet. Maybe I should have. They seem happy with their dogs, their cats or an orange fish swimming round and round in its bowl. People say goldfish are suicidal, that they dive head first out of the water so as to die, just like that, on a marble mantelpiece.

It's crossed my mind, of course, a few times. But I've never seriously considered it. It takes guts to kill yourself. I've never been really tempted. I try to put it out of my mind. I have a sort of self-preservation instinct that makes me think of something else. I don't need any external stimulation, my little thoughts are enough to make me forget my woes.

They say you have to let it all out, that you have to pour out your troubles, talk about them to people around you, think about your neuroses, about the role your parents played. I don't know. So long as I can forget, park all that in a corner, far away from my mind, locked away in a metal box, I'm actually fine. I don't go there. Maybe you think I don't have the courage. What a cheek! I can't live any other way. So it's fine with me if I don't have the courage, repress things in my subconscious or in a corner of the room. I don't want to analyse myself. I don't give a stuff about my case. My case bores me.

So I watch, I try to understand. I watch the streets and my neighbours' apartments. I watch the old people in the métro and the cars going past. All that teeming humanity – which doesn't need me to teem – keeps me entertained.

∽

I rest my shoulders against the traffic light. I know these lights too well. It's my patch, next to the Quick burger place, at the bottom of Rue d'Amsterdam. An intersection's a good spot, there are twice as many people going past. The poor girls in the Bois de Boulogne have the mud to contend with. I prefer the pavement. I'm part of it from top to toe. It's my life. My heart has taken on its colour. It's grey and worn. My soul sweats the filth of the city. People crush out their cigarettes and spit out their chewing gum on it. Sometimes they drop money. They spit on it, but most of all, they trample my soul, sweep it and roll on it too. They tap on it while listening to music. They hurry over me, sometimes lingering for a while when the weather's nice. The sky rains on it, hails on it. My soul is by turns scorching when it's hot, or covered in ice when it snows. It's beginning to warp. There are widening cracks which will eventually swallow it up.

I am the spirit of Notre Dame pacing the Rue d'Amsterdam. That sounds like a song.

Jean-Paul

My parents are so provincial, thinks Jean-Paul. Father all whiskers and Mother with her plump calves. And they're the ones who are choosing the chairs and tables, the stools and the colour of the walls! It's not fair. It's supposed to be our bar, mine and Antoine's, and just because it's their money, they're choosing everything. What do they know about image? What do they know about trends? They'd be better off staying in Nogent to look after the Balto. The suburbs is what they're made for, not a Paris bar.

Even though he's young, Jean-Paul knows the bar scene. He's been working his arse off in it for six years. The youngest manager in the 7th *arrondissement*! That's pretty cool!

But it's always the same old story, his parents will never trust him. So they spend hours arguing over the chairs and tables, the stools and the colour of the walls. They sit there, Father, Mother, Antoine and Jean-Paul, stupidly flicking through the glossy catalogue and niggling over the prices, colours and fabrics. At least Father has a sense of occasion, he smokes his pipe and watches it all with a superior air as if it's a playground fight. Antoine, his brother, says nothing, dull as ditchwater. Mother's the worst, she won't budge an inch, she insists on her Perspex tables with her big gob full of molars, she's like a dog with a bone. Perspex is easier to clean, I tell you. Crap! She wants Perspex because it's cheap. But Jean-Paul won't give in either. He wants wood and metal in his bar, like they have at Costes.

～

At one time, he wanted to be an artist, the persona appealed to him. He had greasy hair and smoked roll-ups. But he likes money so he decided to do bar work. Paid every night – cash in hand, thank you very much. He's seen some things in his twenty-five years, he has! The café world is a different world, as he often says. At night, of course he's tired, but he's content with his life. He was made manager – he no longer has to wear an apron. Now it's a white shirt and fat tie, much better.

He has more money in his pocket but there are responsibilities. The buck stops with him. Keep an eye on the waiters, watch the till, lock up every night and open up every morning. It's been two years. He's slaving his arse off, but he doesn't think about it. When he's not working, he sleeps.

He's about to leave his job and open a café with Antoine – a present from their parents. It's at Convention and is called L'Épervier. He can already picture it, a bar that'll be a magnet for chicks, the cutest ones for him – one of the perks of being the boss. Antoine will be joint owner, but it's not the same, he's Jean-Paul's younger brother, he's never been a manager. Antoine's always been a follower. At school, his enemies were Jean-Paul's. He cultivated his personality alongside his brother's, slightly in the wings, a little in the shadow, his understudy. At the rear, you're not required to think, you take care of the provisions and the wounded. No glory for those who deal with the women, the children and the elderly. No monuments, no associations, only fear and hunger, the smell of mould and of a barn at the bottom of the garden.

⌒

Antoine used to be fat. It still shows a little, he has love handles and his shirt doesn't quite tuck into his trousers. He's slightly shorter than his brother, of smaller build too. He's often been told he's good-looking, but that doesn't help pull the chicks. They're never interested in him. If they do talk to him, it's only to catch Jean-Paul's eye. It doesn't annoy him, he's used to it. He's confident that one day he'll find the woman of his dreams, a Russian dancer. She'll love him, she'll caress his love handles, they'll go for a spin in his car and bathe in rivers. When Antoine can't sleep, he thinks about her. He calls her Melody. He doesn't really have a clear picture of her face but he knows he'd recognize her if he met her. He'd like to work with her, set up a business and buy a modern house. Happiness that smells of mashed potato and chestnuts on a Sunday afternoon. A glass of Coke by the fireside, a cigarette that tastes different when it's raining outside. He and Melody are nice and warm; they smoke and sip Coke. Outside, it's raining. They're shielded from hard knocks, sadness and bankruptcy. Ultimately, they're not asking for much. Antoine dreams of leisure and a leather sofa, work during the week and Frisbee at the weekend. A pretty wife, two curly-haired kids and a decent coffee after lunch.

❧

Jean-Paul's ambition is fired by the movies. On the

road with Faye Dunaway, afraid of neither God nor man. A passionate affair laced with cocaine and champagne, and an automatic gun. Something violent that wrenches your guts and rips out your stomach. Life at 130 mph in a convertible, smashed plates on the floor and Virginia cigarettes. Pain, addiction, a broken heart and hollow cheeks. The idea of mouldering in a little provincial house and listening to the radio like his parents fills him with horror.

In that respect, Antoine and Jean-Paul are very different. Even though they had the same upbringing, the same bike crashes racing down the hill next to their house, the same school, the same football team and the same mates. There's only a year between them. So people say it's their nature, that a person's predestined for heroism or the petty bourgeoisie.

∽

Right now, there's no question of an American shoot-out or a cosy fireside. They're busy choosing tables and chairs, bar stools and the colour of the walls. L'Épervier opens in one month. No time to waste, negotiate with Mother without coming out of it too badly and reach an agreement. It's a strategic battle – strength and diplomacy, the weapons of victory. Patience, compromise, Perspex tables, aluminium tables. Taupe, red, brown, purple, tempered steel, marble, armchairs or sofa, Pastis, Ricard, Stella, Corona, Pelforth, pastries, croissants, buns. Perspex tables, aluminium tables.

∽

Végétal is a weird surname to be lumbered with. Jean-Paul Végétal, Antoine Végétal. They'd both love to change it. But you have no say on the subject of the name you're given. It's the burden of being born. Antoine and Jean-Paul's burden. It's a bit of a handicap. It's not really heavy, more like a huge empty box that they don't know how to carry. Végétal is cumbersome. They were mercilessly bullied at school because of their name.

Their father never seemed to have had a problem with it. Végétal is a name, it doesn't mean anything. I don't understand why you take it so badly. Would you rather have been called Porcher or Chevrolet? I don't see what you've got against our name. I like it, it sounds healthy. Everyone eats organic these days, we're very fashionable, my boy. It's even lucky, being called Végétal; people find it reassuring. I can hear them saying, 'A Végétal can't be bad, they're sweet, the two little Végétal boys, they're gentle, they're fresh, you could eat them!' You should be proud, my sons. It's a gift from your ancestors. My poor father would turn in his grave if he could hear you. You're lucky he was always a bit deaf. The Végétals, a family of workers, deeply attached to their land. You're disparaging our family lineage, my boys. Lestrange? Do you think Lestrange is any better? Végétal's your name and you should be proud of it. Bleed for it! Get your face smashed in defending Végétal! Good God, have some guts, boys. A Végétal doesn't allow people to walk all over him. A Végétal will never allow himself to be trampled on. So don't ever let me catch you whining like sissies again. It's your name, it's beautiful, wear it like a flag. And if you don't like it, that's tough.

Father often made scenes like this. When Antoine and Jean-Paul were little, it scared the pants off them. But it boosted their morale. They set off for school prouder than ever. It was true: Végétal is better than Lestrange! We're not going to let people walk all over us, are we, Antoine? We're not going to let people trample us! We're going to shove their faces in their sauerkraut. Who do those scumbags think they are? Stupid numb-skulls! Go and eat your puke like those fucking

Lestranges! Yesss, nice one, Jean-Paul, let them eat their puke, those fucking Lestranges! Like those poor ... huh ... like those poor Lestranges.

～

The day is over. They call a truce to the negotiations. Mother has the upper hand. Jean-Paul thinks that actually the Perspex isn't so bad. They put away the glossy catalogue. Jean-Paul would like to empty his mind once and for all. We'll see tomorrow.

'Have you got coffee?'

'That's not something I'm asked very often. I'll make you one. Do you want sugar?'

'Yes.'

She brings a cup, a sugar lump, coffee.

'Thank you. You know, coffee's my life.'

'I have a coffee in the morning.'

'I work in a café. It's hard work. You're on your feet all day. It must be the same for you …'

I don't know why I'm thinking of this. When I was a kid, at my grandparents', we always ate the bread from the day before. We had to finish it up, even though there was fresh bread. We never got to eat that.

❧

I don't feel too bad this evening. I've seen worse, believe me. No, this evening, things are OK. I did the same things, said the same words as usual. I'm an old hand, like a factory worker on a production line. The same action, relentlessly, for years. No hope. A little factory worker of the flesh. My factory is the city, my production line, cocks.

❧

Time passes. One more and then I'm going home. Before I go to bed, I'll have something to eat. Something sweet.

Then, like every evening, I'll go and fill up my plastic bottle on the landing. I'll have a lick and a promise at the sink. Have to wait till tomorrow for a shower.

I'll be tired, but I won't sleep. I'll have to numb my mind with television. Something really smutty that makes me feel alive again.

Robert

1

Robert is a sponge. He soaks up events and people, retaining everything in his thick yellow foam. But at some point, if someone grabs him, if he's crushed in the métro or in a cinema queue, he spews out everything in a stream of insults and platitudes, an uncontrolled performance that splatters the toes of your shoes. But he's discreet, people don't notice him. Only don't wring him like a dirty sock, don't squeeze him too hard.

He scrubs away the days and the years, and at the same time he mops up sorrows and regrets. He quite enjoys his condition, it's just that he doesn't like being left in the sink. He deserves better, he has a teaching qualification. Robert's thing had been philosophy. And then he stopped, he can't remember why. Robert's a bit floppy, he has difficulty moving. Sometimes he wants to. He sits down and thinks about it, and finally he stays put. He used to have a lovely armchair in cracked leather. He realized there was a danger that he'd never get up again. He threw it out and has sat on

a wooden chair ever since. It's not as comfortable
but even so he can sit in it for hours. People have
to understand that he's not playing games, that
if he does nothing it is principally an ambition,
like his own personal regurgitated philosophy,
a version of Lettrism. Robert doesn't work. He'll
never work. The only problem is that he doesn't
create anything either. He's never been any good
with his hands or his mind. Robert is a sponge,
he absorbs everything that flows around him. And
that's all.

෴

Being a sponge rather suits him. Or rather, it
appears to suit him because he never questions
whether it does or not. Sometimes he loses his
temper, on one occasion he threw out his aunt's
ancient Chesterfield. In short, his life is running
smoothly. He feels that nothing should be changed.

Robert fancies himself as a leading Surreal-
ist figure or something similar. He could happily
have been a burglar too, or a pirate. That's classy,
not like all those office jobs, four-colour ballpoints
and double-sided adhesive tape.

෴

Robert likes Bryan Ferry and nettle soup. He likes nibbling the bits of cuticle that grow on his nails, falling asleep listening to the radio and flicking through mail order catalogues. Robert likes all that, he's almost a complete wimp. There's something singular about him, something touching. He has dark circles under his eyes, as if his tears had gradually encrusted themselves around his eye sockets. Yes, that's it, the tears furrowed his flesh and turned it purple as they dried. A trace of dried sadness around his eyes. Something that won't pass, always ready to spurt out for some unknown reason. That's Robert's little mystery. He has a secret, a scar he can't show, even though it's raw and always will be. That gaping wound will remain inside him as long as he lives. 'Don't shake me, I'm full of tears', he might have said had he been a genius and a famous writer called Henri Calet.

~

What am I without other people? asks Robert. I mean, if there weren't any other people, would I wash my hands after going to the toilet? No, definitely not, he wouldn't wash his hands, he wouldn't change his socks. He'd crawl on the ground like a little rat full of slime. As Sartre said, the other is the indispensable mediator between myself and me. But Robert is no Calet, and he's no Sartre either. No, I definitely wouldn't wash my hands, I'd eat my bogies and fart in the street.

That's pretty much how Robert suddenly came to realize that he needed others, all those other people around him. He decided to face the world, meet people, sign up for yoga classes. Suddenly, he aspired to a social life, to negotiations, to the hustle and bustle of the crowd. He pounded the pavement, he carried heavy banners with enthusiasm, he went shopping on Saturday afternoons on Boulevard Haussmann. He tried to chat up girls and find friends to play darts with. He bought a TV and burned his books. He became a blinkered activist and chased girls. He found a job and joined a trade union. He wore his jeans like everyone else, he played online poker.

Then he realized that he wasn't made for that life, that he wasn't made for them. He went back to his chair and his solitude. He had never felt so free as at that moment.

He has ten or so bonsais. He calls them dwarf trees. The sales assistant always corrects him, but it's useless, for Robert they'll always be dwarf trees. He's not exactly wrong, it's a good image.

He loves his dwarf trees. He's put some in the bathroom, in his bedroom, and in the living room. He tends them, pruning the branches and watering them every day with a mineral-water spray. He bought them Japanese-style ceramic pots. The dwarf trees deserve them, they're well behaved, they have leaves, they don't grow. He's given them names, but nobody knows that. Dwarfbus, L'il Dwarf, Branched Dwarf, Titch, Lilliput, Mimimati … they seem to like it.

In winter, he turns on the central heating to protect them. He plays them music. When the weather's nice, in summer, he puts them out in the sun on his little balcony, but not for too long, it's bad for the bark. He talks to them sometimes but he's a bit embarrassed about it. So he goes out and tries to forget his dwarf trees, he mills around in the crowd for an afternoon.

When he goes home, he's happy to see them. They're so small! Their leaves so tiny!

At night, when he sleeps, he can hear them breathe. Surrounded by his miniature trees, he feels reassured. You could call it his little secret garden but that would be too corny. It's his little secret garden and he's proud of it. Ridiculous but sincere.

So he loves his little secret garden. He devotes his mornings to tending the tiny leaves and the tiny roots, naked under his dressing gown, a cigarette dangling from his lips.

~

At one point, Robert had wanted to start a novel. Set in the nineteenth century would be nice. Something along the lines of *Lady Chatterley*, a love story against a backdrop of social issues. In the mornings, he sat at the little kitchen table and thought about it. It kept him busy for hours. He had found his calling. He would be a writer. Cursed, of course, it wasn't worth it otherwise. He'd drink black coffee and smoke his lungs away. Yes, that would be good, he'd have tousled hair and sport a cravat and cufflinks. He'd speak with a slightly upper-class accent, he'd be a man of letters. The novel was not progressing, but in the meantime, he cultivated his personal style. A real man of letters, slightly dirty, slightly pedantic. He wanted to suffer outrageously, take drugs, find inspiration, write all night long by candlelight. So much more stylish than a neon lamp. Brown ink, yellowing pages, notebooks in his pockets and stained fingers. He fancied the idea of himself as sad, tormented, hunched over a piece of paper. He bought a pair of owl spectacles and looked for a muse. While waiting for his true muse, the lady of the night who would make him bleed, he made do with Kim Carnes. Sitting on the sleeve of her LP, a gun-toting man beside her. Oh! Kim Carnes! The perfect woman, sitting cross-legged on her velvet sofa. And he listened to 'Bette Davis Eyes', dreaming of her, inhaling her anguished voice deep inside his soul.

The novel began something like this:

'Have you ever noticed,' he said, 'how an empty
cup on your table in a café looks perfectly natural
if it's yours, and dirty, disgusting even, if it was
there when you sat down?'

It was a good idea to start with a real-life incident. But after that he was stuck. That was the end of his career as a scribbler.

He gave up on the idea. He sat on his wooden chair and waited for it to blow over.

2

Robert looks at himself from a distance. He smiles when he pictures himself a few months earlier, obsessed with the idea of being a man of letters, allowing his hair to grow, donning a cravat every morning. Yes, he has a good laugh when he thinks back on that phase. But he's not ashamed, it feels as if it happened to someone else. That man can't be him, that clownish scribbler with cufflinks and a rusty inkwell. No way can that be him. So let's laugh at him because he really is ridiculous.

Robert is able to see himself from a great distance. That is a strength, but it's also a trap. He doesn't recognize himself at all. He sees himself rather in the way that people insist that the curly-headed little boy perched proudly on his tricycle, that little boy in the photograph you're holding, is you, at Grandma's, the summer you were five. You can't be ashamed of him. Of the snot dripping from his nose, it doesn't matter, it's not really you. No memories of that tricycle ride in Grandma's garden. All right, if you're sure it's me, I believe you. But that little boy doesn't affect you. He's cute, there's snot dribbling from his nose. And then what? He's only you because people say so.

That's what Robert feels; he has no need of a photo or of a childhood. His own memories are alien to him.

Today, Robert has bought a new tree. He hasn't named it yet. He certainly intends to find a name for it. We'll see later, he thinks. Right now, he needs something to eat, his rumbling stomach is his main concern. He can't do anything on an empty stomach. Some people can think more clearly when they're hungry, but with him it's the opposite. I'll have a four-cheese pizza. Yes, to take away. That's quick! Yes, of course, it's because you're Italian, how silly of me!

He eats his pizza at the little kitchen table and gradually his head fills with dwarf tree names. He's made up his mind, it will be Billy the Kid. That sounds cool, as if he'd bought it in the USA. A little tree from Houston, Texas. A tree with cowboy boots and a gun. Now that *is* cool! The next one will be a Mexican, he'll dress it in a little poncho and a big hat. Oh, his little trees are so lovely! If he looks after them well, they'll outlive him. It'll be his opus, his mark. But who will he leave his dwarf trees to? Who would be prepared to take them into their living room as if they were their own children, water them with a mineral-water spray and prune the superfluous little branches? Bah, he'll find someone. For the time being, he's looking after them, and he's happy.

It's his tender loving care that keeps them alive.

They don't grow, of course, but they are nourished by it. They drink Robert's little attentions like their own sap, the blood that courses through their veins. It's an image – Robert knows full well that they're not people. That's why he loves them, like an elderly spinster with her cats.

Robert doesn't despise people. Most of the time, he forgives them excessively. It's just that he doesn't know how to relate to them. He's a bit gauche, he's unable to interest people or make them laugh. So he sits on his wooden chair and waits patiently, as always.

But what is he waiting for? He doesn't know, it feels like a void to be plugged. Which stopper should he use? He'd have been extremely grateful if only someone had helped him, told him what to do. But there you go, no one had ever been there for him. Robert had built himself, like a slightly wobbly house. The foundations aren't very stable, the roof's falling in, he is less and less able to withstand the assaults of the wind and rain. One day, he'll collapse. All those tiles crumbling will be like a rock fall. There'll be nothing left but the bare rafters, intersecting beams that no longer support anything. A ruined Robert, his carcass naked like a common laboratory skeleton. Medical students will stick a cigar in his jaw, they'll make him give the two-fingered salute and arrange his pelvis in a suggestive posture. It's understandable, it's not a person they'll be seeing, only a frame, an assembly of bones placed end to end, a human-sized jigsaw puzzle whose pieces have complicated Latin names that you have to learn if you want to pass your exams. He'll give those cheeky students grief. He'll be called Oscar and wear a bowler hat.

He retains all that in his yellow foam.

He has moved the little wooden chair over to the window. There's a man on the other side of the street. He's leaning against the railings in his shirtsleeves, smoking. He doesn't really seem to be paying attention to what's happening around him. He's not interested in the goings-on of the street. He smokes. He's thinking of something important. He scratches his head. Is his wife cheating on him? His mother dying? Have his shares taken a nose-dive? It must be something of the sort, he looks very anxious.

Robert watches the man at the same time as drinking in the life of the street. The stallholders shout the prices of vegetables and fish. Women walk about, leeks poking out of their shopping baskets. They're getting in provisions, as people used to say during the war. When Robert thinks about it fleetingly, he'd quite like a war. He imagines himself as a Resistance fighter, shooting at the enemy from high up in his apartment. Concealed behind the window, holding a rifle with telescopic sight. Unimaginable bravery defending his little trees. But it's peacetime, he's not exactly going to take pot shots at housewives with shopping caddies. So he watches them and tries to guess what they'll be cooking for lunch. What can you make with leeks and a baguette?

From time to time, he spots a bottle of red poking out of a basket. The sound of the cork popping before lunch. He crooks his finger and makes a popping sound in his cheek. Pop. Pop. Another bottle that'll course through our veins. We need to forget for a while, we need to get drunk when we've got nothing better to do. It's the fruit of our land that we're drinking. Pop. The bottle neck clinks against the sides of the glasses. It can't be bad, we say to your good health before drinking. We don't say cirrhosis or alcoholism, no, we say to your good health, so come on, let's have a drink to celebrate! After all, what's the problem? We drown our sorrows where we please.

～

The bustling street makes him restless. All those

housewives out and about, all those cars, all those kids on scooters. Go out, that's a good idea. Slip on a jacket, it's not cold today. This one will do. Close the window. Mustn't forget my keys, whatever happens. In my pocket. Cell phone. No one will call but take it anyway. Also in my pocket. There, I'm ready. Oh yes, shoes. Quick, the fresh air's calling. Shoelaces. Faster, for Chrissakes! Get out. Get out. Escape from the daily gloom, walk through the streets of the 14th *arrondissement*. A little expedition on foot. Dogs, passing women, mopeds.

How about taking the métro?

'What are you going to do?'

'I don't know, sweetheart!' (Laughter) 'You're the boss.'

'Can I ask for anything I want?'

'If you've got the money. As far as I'm concerned, you know …'

'I haven't got much money.'

'So we'll make do with what you've got.'

I'm done for the night. The money comes fast. At what cost?

Back to the Zenith Hotel. Always the same old routine. I climb the six flights of stairs up to my dismal room with the paint peeling off the walls. The stairs are worn down in the centre from too many feet tramping up and down them in boots or trainers. I don't like this stairwell. I hurry to the top.

I unlock the door with my big gilt key, then slump down on my little bed and lie there, on my back, my legs dangling, still dressed, the strap of my bag around my arm. I'd like to be able to stay like this forever – as flat as a pancake. I feel good. I think of nothing.

But I have to sit up. Mentally I count. On thirty, I'll get up. Twenty-seven … twenty-eight … twenty-nine … thirty. Right, another two minutes. I count again. I don't want to get up. Twenty-seven … twenty-eight … twenty-nine … thirty …

〜

Slowly I take off my make-up. I wipe cotton wool over my face with one hand, holding a small fragment of mirror in the other.

I ignore my reflection. I've given up looking for crow's feet around my eyes and new blackheads on my nose. I think about other things – I don't want to see myself.

❧

Slowly, I get undressed. I let my clothes drop gently on to the white-tiled floor. I don't fold them, they're dirty. I'm going to the launderette tomorrow, as I do every week.

I slip into my nightie. That's my evening routine. My movements are mechanical, like in the morning when I scratch my head and make coffee.

My routine makes me forget the nasty taste seeping through my body. I concentrate on the moment. I slip into my nightie and go and fill my water bottle on the landing.

I go back to my room and smoke a cigarette in silence.

❧

I double-lock the door. At last I can go to bed, turn on the television and light up another fag.

I gently fall asleep, watching people living on the other side of the screen.

The commentators' voices are soothing. They have that journalistic tone that makes them sound beautiful and professional. The voices of those who keep us informed.

I trust that voice. It isn't nasty. I can let myself go.

I listen with one ear. With the other, the one that's glued to the pillow, I start to nod off. A pleasant voice with a journalistic tone.

I fall asleep. Tomorrow's another day.